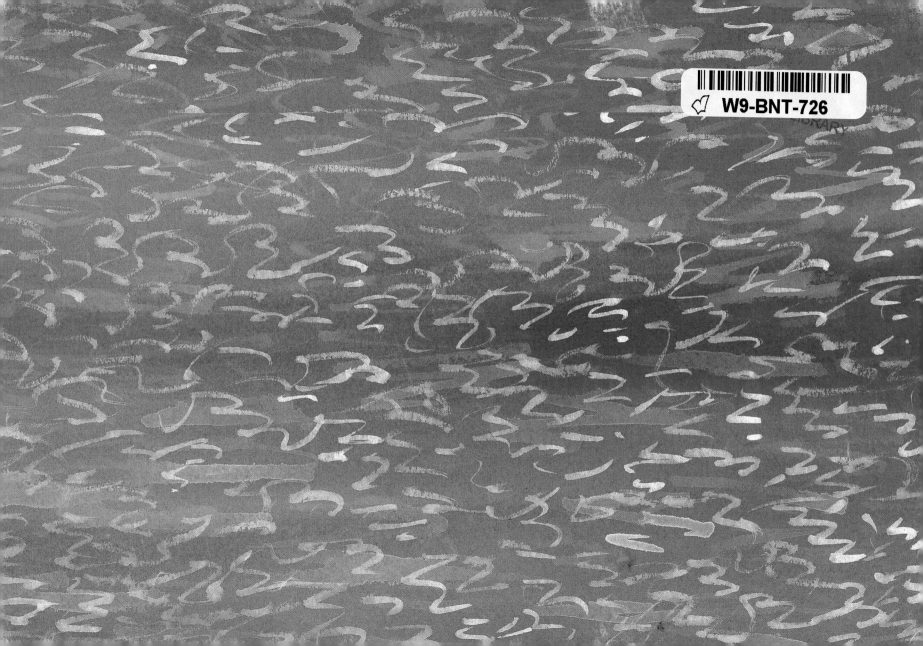

For beach lovers

Atheneum Books for Young Readers
An imprint of Simon & Schuster Children's Publishing Division
1230 Avenue of the Americas
New York, New York 10020

Book design by Ann Bobco
The text of this book is set in Deepdene.
The illustrations are rendered in watercolor.

First Edition
Printed in Hong Kong by South China Printing Co. (1988) Ltd.
10   9   8   7   6   5   4   3

Library of Congress Cataloging-in-Publication Data
Mathers, Petra.
Lottie's new beach towel / written and illustrated by Petra Mathers.—1st ed.
p.   cm.
"An Anne Schwartz book."
Summary: Lottie the chicken has a number of adventures at the
beach, during which her new towel comes in handy.
ISBN 0-689-81606-5
[1. Chickens—Fiction. 2. Beaches—Fiction. 3. Towels—Fiction.]
I. Title. Pz7.M42475Lo   1998
[E]—dc21   97-6689

Lottie's New Beach Towel

Lottie
Crookroad
Oysterville

by petra mathers

An Anne Schwartz Book
ATHENEUM BOOKS FOR YOUNG READERS

Lottie was squeezing lemons when a package arrived.

Inside was a beach towel with a note.

"How lovely," said Lottie, "and just in time for my picnic with Herbie."

It was a beautiful summer day.

The sun was high and the sand was hot.
Soon Lottie's feet were on fire.

She hopped onto the cooler. *Now what?*

The towel! Put the towel in front,
hop off the cooler onto the towel.

Put the cooler in front.
Hop off the towel onto the cooler.
Towel, cooler, off, on . . .

all the way down to the water.
"Ahhhh."

"Here I am, come and get me!

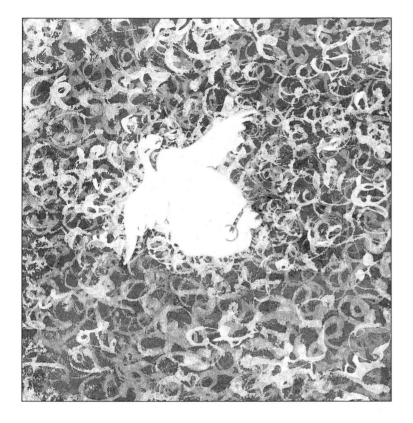

Is that my foot?
Silly me, it's a starfish."

"Now I get to try my new beach towel.

Whoa, I better turn ar—

. . . rrumph."
"Ahoy, Lottie," shouted Herbie. "Hop aboard."

They headed for Pudding Rock.
"The motor sounds funny," said Lottie.
"I think it's just tired," said Herbie.

"I think it just went to sleep,"
said Lottie.

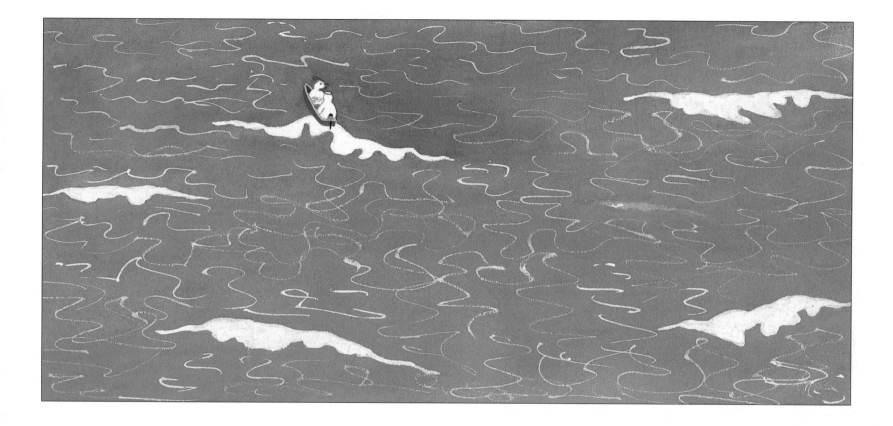

What now?

The towel!
"Hard to lee, Lottie," said Herbie. "I see a perfect place for a picnic."
"Aye aye, captain," said Lottie.

"I'm so hungry I don't care if there is *sand*
 on my sandwich. Get it, Lottie?"
"Yes, Herbie, and jelly on your belly."

"Lottie, look, a ghost!" cried Herbie.
"I hear voices," whispered Lottie.

"Come back! Oh, please come back!"
"Stop that veil!"
But the veil flew on.

"Gone," cried the bride.
"But darling, we can still get married,"
    said the groom.

"What now, what now?" sobbed the
    flower girl.

"My towel," said Lottie. "It would look pretty with your dress."

After the wedding there was a party.

They all ate a lot of cake.
Especially Herbie.

"Oh Lottie, my stomach feels tight.
Will my feathers pop off?" he asked.
"Time to go home," said Lottie.

Everyone else was leaving, too.
The motor started without trouble.

The new friends waved to each other until they were specks on the water.

The boat reached Lottie's dune by moonlight.

"So long, mate," said Herbie. "I had a whale of a day."
"Me too, Herbie. Good night," said Lottie.

She walked up the dune. The cool sand squeaked between her toes.

Still full of wedding cake, Lottie skipped
dinner and sat down to write a letter. . . .

Dear Aunt Mattie,
Thank you so much for my new
beach towel. Without it I
might be in the hospital with
burnt feet or lost at sea with
Herbie. There might not even
have been a wedding. But let
me start at the beginning.

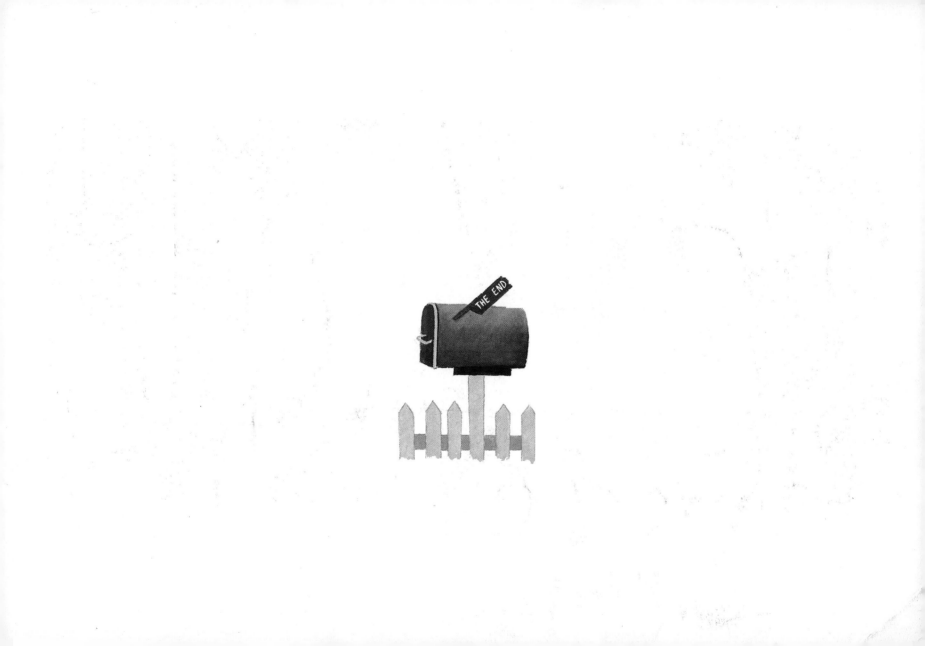

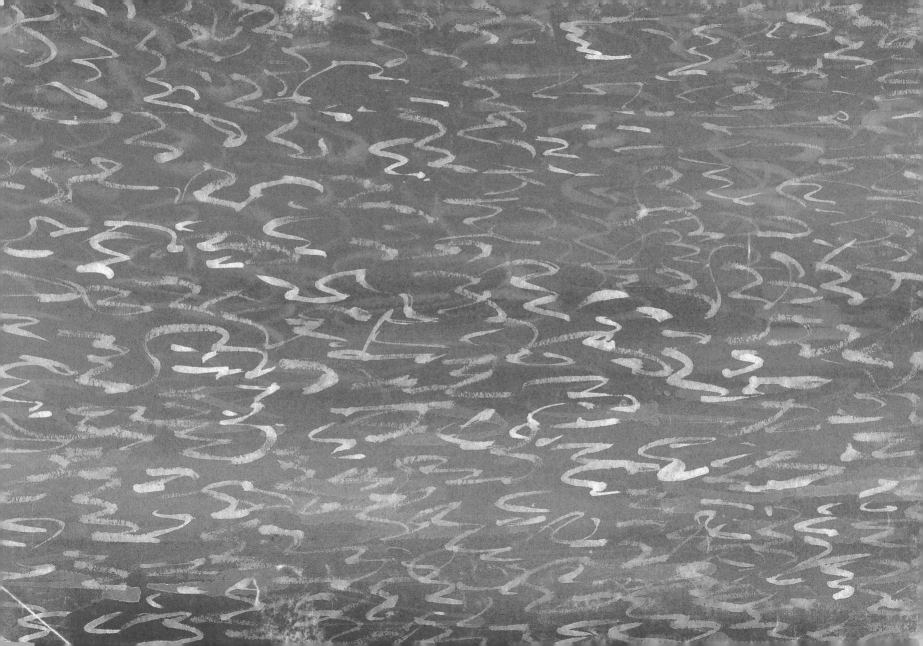